Greg and the Barbarian

SHERILE REILLY

Suite 300 – 990 Fort Street
Victoria, BC, Canada V8V 3K2
www.friesenpress.com

First Edition — 2014

ISBN
978-1-4602-3508-9 (Hardcover)
978-1-4602-3509-6 (Paperback)
978-1-4602-3510-2 (eBook)

1. Juvenile Fiction, General

Distributed to the trade by The Ingram Book Company

For Mom: Dreams become reality

ACKNOWLEDGEMENTS

Thanks to Mike Reilly, Ed Reilly,
Betty Eileen Bruerton and Donna Tunney.
Thanks to my sixth-grade students who inspired me.
Thanks to Marlene Dunn for her many suggestions.
Thanks to Ted Williams for the final edit.

Greg and the Barbarian

CHAPTER ONE

The noon hour bell blasted. Classroom doors banged open and groups of fifth and sixth-grade students scattered into the hall. Greg's runners squeaked as he dodged from one side to the other, trying to avoid a collision. Lunch kits thumping against the walls mixed with loud voices and scurrying footsteps as the students darted to the lunchroom and exit doors. Greg Hutchins veered to the wall.

"Ouch." Greg winced as he touched the bump on his head. "You big bully," he muttered.

Yesterday the Barbarian had used his plastic lunch bucket to wallop Greg. Caught by surprise, he'd been too stunned to strike back. The lunchroom supervisor had stepped in just in time to save him from really being pounded.

Dragging his feet, Greg rounded the corner and stopped. He stared at some drawings of large dragons.

Whack! A door bumped open.

Elbowing and pushing, two boys stumbled in front of Greg.

"Race you," one of them yelled.

"Hey, wait for me." The second boy scrambled to his feet and pelted down the hall.

Once the noisy crowd cleared, Greg peered into the cloakroom. Where was Tommy? They always went to the lunchroom together, but today Greg wasn't in any rush to get there. Yesterday the Barbarian's parting words had been, "I'll get you." The Barbarian was big and strong, and mean enough to make it happen. Slumping against the wall, Greg sighed. He'd rather be anyplace else.

"Hi, Greg." Tommy appeared in the doorway. "Come on, let's go. I'm starved."

Greg didn't move.

Tommy frowned, "Still worried about the Barbarian?"

"Yeah." Greg nodded.

"What are you going to do?"

Greg shrugged. "I don't know. But you better go or you'll be late."

"Okay." Tommy started down the hall. He glanced back and gave Greg a thumbs-up.

Greg tried to smile back, but he really didn't feel like it so he waved. Moving closer to the bulletin board, he studied the drawings again, admiring one picture—a dragon. Its scales were carefully drawn and its claws gripped the rocks. But only about a third was finished and the paper crumpled. It looked as if someone had crunched it up and afterwards changed his mind and tried to flatten it. But who'd drawn it? He couldn't see a name in the corner. Strange.

"Hi, Greg," came a teacher's voice.

He jumped and turned to see Miss Clark.

"You'd better hurry or you'll miss attendance."

Greg wanted to ask her if she knew who'd done the drawing but she smiled at him and continued down the long corridor, the tapping of her heels growing fainter. He liked her; she taught art, his favorite subject.

Trying to figure out a way to avoid the Barbarian, Greg paused and gazed at the orange-colored doors and an idea hit him. Why not eat outside? Nobody would see him if he found a place to hide, and maybe by Monday the Barbarian would forget all about him.

Gee, the littlest thing seemed to send the Barbarian into orbit. All he'd done yesterday was tell the guy he was 'dumb'. What was so bad about that?

Three exit doors were close by. Escape would be easy. Tiptoeing to the closest one, Greg slowly pushed down the bar and squeezed through.

In one jump, he cleared the four steps and landed on the sidewalk. Crouching on his hands and knees, he held his lunch kit with his teeth and crawled between the building and the bushes. The sun glistened on the white stuccoed wall, warming him and he leaned back. He balanced his lunch kit on his legs and snapped open the lid. On top was a handy-wipe, as usual, and he scrubbed his hands, getting rid of most of the dirt.

Peanut butter and strawberry jelly. "Mm…good," murmured Greg.

Large crumbs dropped from his lap onto the ground. Ants scurried about, trying to pick them up. One little ant wrestled with a piece three times its body size. After four attempts, the ant finally lifted the gigantic crumb and struggled to move forward.

"Gotcha." Greg placed his foot in front of the ant, forcing it to stop. The piece of bread toppled. "Let's see you get out of this."

Not content to leave its newly found prize, the ant lifted the crumb again and tried to move in a different direction.

"Take that." Greg stamped his foot in front of the ant, pretending it was the Barbarian. "You'll never ever push me again. I'll get you." He'd love to squash Fred Farley, better known as the Barbarian. If the Barbarian was an ant, he'd cover him with dirt and never have to see him again.

After a few minutes of blocking the ant's path, Greg let it carry the crumb away and he relaxed. "Ahhh," he sighed.

Thump.

Greg froze. A runner slapped against the pavement.

Thump-thump.

Scrunching down, Greg tried to make himself smaller. "Please don't let anyone find me," he whispered and strained to hear.

Silence.

Maybe they'd missed him from the lunchroom and a teacher or, worse still, the principal was looking for him. How would he explain being outside? He'd be in big trouble for sure. The leaves above his head rustled and the branches shook. Who was there? Why didn't they talk?

Slowly Greg lifted his head and glanced up, his heart slammed against his chest. Directly above him loomed the Barbarian with a snarl on his big, ugly face. He looked like a mad dog, only meaner.

The Barbarian glared at Greg. "You're dead, shrimp."

Greg froze. What was he going to do? How could he get out of the bushes?

He was trapped.

"I'm gonna make you eat dirt. Think you'll like it?" The barbarian sneered, his wild, sandy-colored hair swishing back and forth.

Greg wiggled to his left. Maybe, just maybe, he'd get far enough out of the Barbarian's reach and make a run for it.

With one push, the Barbarian shoved the branches aside.

Greg cringed as a big hand reached down.

A loud voice rang from the parking lot. "Get out of there. What are you kids doing playing behind the bushes?"

Whew! Greg had never been so glad to hear anyone's voice in his life. It was Mr. Sanders, the school caretaker. The Barbarian scowled at Greg as he crawled out and onto the grass. "You wait, shrimp. I'll get you."

Greg snapped the lid on his lunch kit and got up, brushing the back of his jeans. He stepped on the sidewalk where Mr. Sanders was waiting and shaking his head.

"Kids," he muttered. "Hurry up, the bell's going to ring. And remember, I'll be keeping my eye on you all the way.

Greg nodded and scrambled around the corner of the school. He glanced back. The caretaker was still there. It'd been close, too close. The Barbarian almost clobbered him.

Hurrying down the compound, Greg saw everyone pushing and shoving, trying to be first. Greg's face twisted in disgust as he stayed at the back of the line. From his place he watched the fourth-graders line up near the wall on the right side of the entrance doors.

"Give it to me." A small boy darted from the line and stretched to get his baseball cap from a bigger student.

"Catch it," yelled the tall boy. The hat sailed high in the air.

"Go get it, go get it," chanted the other kids.

"Let me have it." The small child reached, but the tall boy snatched the cap out of the air and held it high above his head.

"Come and get it," he taunted and waved the cap.

The fourth-grader jumped, but each time the big kid stretched a little higher and the small boy's face reddened as he made another frantic leap.

"Reach for it."

Greg's face burned. It wasn't fair when big guys picked on little guys. It just wasn't fair.

Before he thought about what he was doing, Greg raced towards the blue cap as it sailed high in the air again. He leapt and snatched it, then thrust the cap into the little boy's hand.

The buzzer blared.

The door opened and Mr. Peabody appeared. Quiet and in a single file the students entered the building.

"Greg," called Miss Clark as she came towards him. "Please set up the projector for me when you come to art class."

"Sure, Miss Clark," Greg replied.

In the cloakroom Frank asked, "Hey, done any more cartoons?"

"Not lately," answered Greg.

"You should do one of Peabody." Frank laughed.

"All right everybody, line up." The teacher's voice cut through the noise.

Greg picked up his supplies and headed for the back door where Mr. Peabody stood. With his long pointed nose, bald head with a little hair on the side, and funny-looking bow tie, he'd be a great subject for a cartoon drawing.

At the entrance to the art room, Miss Clark welcomed them and Greg hurried to move the projector in front of the screen.

"Thanks, Greg." He sat in his seat and Miss Clark said, "today we'll start with something new." Everyone watched while she put a transparency on the machine and drew a circle.

Greg stared at it. This wasn't like Miss Clark. Usually her art periods were fun. The students moaned.

"Be patient. I know one circle isn't very interesting but if I add a few more lines and shapes I can change a plain circle into something interesting. And, I'm doing this without the aid of a computer program. Yes, I know it's easy to get everything from the computer, but I want to show you what you can create by yourselves and after, if you want to find other ways to enhance your own drawings, use the computer."

Miss Clark drew a fuzzy, little caterpillar with a big grin on his face. Next she added a background of leaves and branches.

"Now, I'll start again and this time you copy me step by step." Miss Clark drew another shape.

Greg picked up his pen. Wow, he had a great idea for a new cartoon.

When the students were finished, Miss Clark said, "Greg, how'd you like to come up and sketch something for us?"

Greg gulped and got up slowly.

"Draw something easy," whispered Frank as Greg walked to the front of the room where Miss Clark handed him a pen.

"Please show us one of your little cartoons? Start with a basic shape and demonstrate your steps."

The bright light from the projector shone in his eyes and he gazed out at his classmates who watched and waited.

His mind went blank.

CHAPTER TWO

Greg swallowed and started to draw a circle. The heat from the projector made him feel warm and his hands were damp as he gripped the felt pen.

Looking up from the glaring, white light, Greg tried to see the other kids but their faces were dark and silent. What if they thought his drawing was stupid?

Clutching the pen, he carefully drew a head, arms and feet for a little duck. For the final touch he sketched a tiny vest. Nobody made a sound and Greg gulped. Sweat trickled from his forehead down the side of his face. He put the pen down, and returned to his seat.

"Good job," whispered Frank.

Miss Clark walked to the front. "See, Greg has created a new cartoon character."

Greg relaxed and heaved a sigh of relief.

"Now, let's see what each of you can do. If you want, you may copy Greg's work. Do you have a name for your duck, Greg?" asked Miss Clark.

He sat up straight and answered, "Dapper Duck."

"I like the name." Miss Clark printed the words on the transparency.

* * *

At the end of the day, Greg shuffled down the hall. Now, if he could get home without seeing the Barbarian. Maybe the big bully would get struck by lightning over the weekend and on Monday everyone in his class would be standing in little groups and talking about the Barbarian's horrible fate. Greg pictured himself explaining…

"Lightning is formed when positive and negative electrical charges flow toward one another. The spark they make is the lightning we see."

Angela would say, "Oh, Greg, you're so smart. You know more than anyone in the school about science."

Feeling five inches taller, Greg would explain, "Lightning has great power to destroy, and this is what the Barbarian didn't realize." He'd shake his head to emphasize the point. "Staying under a tree. How foolish."

"Wanna come to my house?"

Greg blinked and the imaginary circle of students disappeared. Tommy stood right beside him, with a funny expression on his face.

Still thinking about the Barbarian, Greg didn't answer. He knew his mother would scold him for such thoughts.

"You never know what his home life is like," she repeated when he complained to her.

"But Mom, you don't know him. He's big, mean and ugly."

Greg recalled their talk and his mom's reply, "Perhaps he feels ugly, and that's why he acts like he does."

"Come on, let's go." Tommy started towards the exit.

"Where?" Greg gazed at Tommy.

"Man, you're really out of it."

"Sorry, Tommy."

"Ah, forget the Barbarian for the weekend. Maybe his dad will get transferred and we'll never see him again."

They both laughed and Greg doubted it. The Barbarian would still be there on Monday.

They raced out of the schoolyard.

"What are you doing tonight?" asked Tommy.

"Can't play," replied Greg, jogging beside his best friend.

"Why?" Tommy slowed down.

Greg shrugged. "Mom told me to come straight home. She said they had a surprise."

Tommy wrinkled his nose. "Weird. I wonder what's happening."

"Don't know. It sounded pretty important, but Mom said I'd have to be patient until tonight."

CHAPTER THREE

As the Barbarian turned his house key in the lock and pushed open the door, the window pane rattled in its old wooden casing. He wondered when the glass would crash to the floor. Stepping into the back hall, he dropped his backpack on the clothes dryer. From the kitchen came the familiar clatter of the fridge.

A blast of cold air smacked Fred's face as he opened the freezer door inside the fridge and searched for a Popsicle. The thick ice on the walls felt cold on his hand. He pushed packages of hamburger and frozen fish and chips aside, but didn't find a Popsicle.

"Darn," he muttered and closed the door.

Glancing at the clock, he decided he'd better get the dishes washed or at least put them in the dishwasher before his dad got home. It wouldn't be so bad if they did the dishes together, but his dad always left him in the kitchen cleaning-up, while he flopped in front of the TV. Fred remembered helping his mother. She'd tell him funny stories about her job and she always asked him questions to help him study for tests.

He was a lot smarter and he wasn't called the Barbarian in his old school. He was Fred Farley. But his mom and dad were always yelling and she'd gone away. He'd got some letters and a few texts promising she'd come back and visit him, but she hadn't, and now he was sure she never would.

"It's not fair." Fred banged his fist on the cupboard. "Why'd you leave us? I never had trouble at my other school." He shoved another glass in the dishwasher and slammed the door. "Look at this house. It's a mess." He hung his head. "And me, too. No wonder they call me the Barbarian."

He'd never been teased before by kids like Greg. Fred smirked at the picture of the shrimp cringing in the bushes. The little coward tried to hide.

"Ha." Fred gritted his teeth. "I almost got you today, shrimp. Teach you to keep your mouth shut."

Remembering he had work to do, he grabbed four potatoes out of the plastic bag on the counter, and peeled them. He dropped the potatoes into a pot of water on the stove. Next he took some pork chops from the fridge and plopped them in the frying pan. If he turned up the heat everything would cook faster and be ready by the time his dad got home.

The chops sizzled and the potatoes boiled as he grabbed his backpack from the dryer, pulled out a book and headed for the sofa in the living room.

He'd read for a few minutes.

Bang.

Fred raised his head and the book fell to the floor. Oh, gosh, his dad was home. What time was it?

"Hey, son, where are you?"

"I'm here." He jumped to his feet and headed for the kitchen. Something was burning. He raced to the stove and clicked off the burner as his dad came in.

"Weren't you paying attention to the supper?" Mr. Farley scowled as he lifted the lid and peered into the pot.

"Sorry, Dad."

Mr. Farley shook his head. "Well, don't stand and gawk. Get them out."

"I'm trying, Dad. I'm trying." With a fork Fred poked at the black potatoes stuck to the bottom of the pot. They fell apart as he dumped half onto his father's plate and the rest on his own.

"Did you think to check the meat?" His dad rolled up his shirt sleeves and washed his hands at the kitchen sink.

"I'm doing it right now," replied Fred. The chops smelled good and when he lifted the lid he saw they were nice and brown.

"Where's the vegetables?"

Darn, he'd forgotten.

"Never learn," muttered his father.

Fred opened the cupboard and pulled out a can of peas, making a face and thinking how mushy they were. His mom had always made salads with lots of tomatoes, lettuce, celery, and mushrooms. Clanging cutlery interrupted his thoughts as his father set the table.

When they both sat down, Fred's father eyed him and said, "So what you do at school today?"

Fred hated the question. What'd his father think he did? He went to classes the same as always. Sometimes he got in trouble, but he never ever told his dad, so he said, "Oh, the usual."

"Play any football?"

"Not today. We didn't have gym."

"Well you know son, you should practise every chance you get. You've the right size and build."

People were always reminding him how big he was. But it didn't mean he wanted to be in the pros like his dad had until he injured his knee. That'd been the end of his career, and now he wanted Fred to play.

"When I was your age, I knew how to toss a ball. If you'd exercise more."

Fred took a deep breath and sucked in his stomach, dreading the lecture about the good old days.

"Ahhh." His dad got a faraway look. "Those were great times."

Well it's not now, Fred longed to scream but instead he interrupted, "You like the chops?"

"Yeah, they're okay. Potatoes taste burned."

"I know." Fred stared at his plate. There were pieces of black on every potato. "Going out tonight, Dad?"

"No. Why?" His father squinted at him. "You want me to leave."

"Nope. I only wondered." Jeez, his dad got mad at everything he said and did tonight. Must've been a bad day at work. It sure seemed like his dad had more bad days than good. Sort of like me in school, thought Fred.

The meal continued in silence.

"What are you doing tonight?" his father asked.

"Well ... uh ..." stammered Fred. "I might read a book."

"Is that all you ever want to do? You're like your mother. Let's go outside and practise passing."

"Oh, no," groaned Fred.

His dad pushed his chair back and stood. "Hurry up and finish your supper. We'll get you in shape."

Fred hoped his father didn't plan on getting him in shape all in one evening. He wished he wasn't quite so big—not as small as the shrimp, Greg, but a little smaller.

He took the dishes to the sink, scraped and rinsed them.

"Hurry up." His dad scooped up several dishes and put them in the sink while Fred scraped the burned pot. "It'll be dark and we won't get much practise. Let's leave the dishes."

His dad went to the bedroom while Fred left the potato pot to soak in soapy water and changed his clothes.

In a few minutes they jogged the five blocks to the park. Panting, Fred slumped against a large tree. His father ran to the far end of the field, the football in his hand.

"Catch," bellowed his dad.

Fred reached for the ball and caught it. He hugged it to his chest and his dad shouted. "Good, now run and throw."

Fred kept on running and made an overhand pass. But it seemed like the ball had only reached his dad when it shot back, smacked him on the arm and bounced to the ground.

He picked it up.

"Run faster." His dad shouted.

Fred slowed, trying to catch his breath.

"Don't stop. Keep running."

Fred gripped the ball and ran.

"Move it, move it. Pass now."

Panting, Fred threw the ball. The pass back was high and wide. Keeping his eyes on it, he veered to the right and stretched his arms. *"Don't drop it. Please don't drop it. Come on, this time you won't fumble."*

"Look out for the trees," boomed a voice in the distance, but Fred's only thought was about the football that was almost in his hands. So close. He'd make a wonderful catch. As he reached for the ball, the toe of his runner hit something and he lurched forward while his left leg caught and didn't move. A sharp pain jolted through his right ankle as he twisted it and crashed to the cold ground. He tried to sit up but the buzzing in his head didn't stop.

"Come on kid. Get up." His dad grabbed his arm and pulled. "A little tumble never hurt any football player."

Darn, his father never quit. Fred took a deep breath and gritted his teeth, aching all over. He wanted to scream. *I'm not a football player and I never want to be one.* He wanted to lie there and cry for a while, but he'd never cry in front of his dad.

"Here, give me your hand. Get back up on your feet."

Using his father for support, he stood and balanced on his left leg. The taste of soggy potatoes and peas burned the back of his throat and his vision blurred.

Strong arms caught and supported him.

"Steady now. You can do it."

"Ow, my ankle." Fred moaned.

"Probably a little sprain. Next time don't run with your eyes closed," said his dad.

"There won't be a next time."

"Sure there will."

"But Dad, I don't like football."

His dad's grip tightened. "Give it a chance. You'll change your mind.'

No, I won't, Fred longed to shout.

"Come on, let's get home. I'll get you an ice pack."

Fred gritted his teeth, clutched his father's arm and hobbled the five blocks to the house. All he wanted to do was get an ice pack and escape to his own bedroom to read.

"Almost there." His dad's tone lightened. "See, you made it. You'll be mended in no time." He patted Fred on the back.

With help from his dad, Fred hopped into the house. Why couldn't his dad understand that he didn't like football and he didn't want to be a pro?

One of these days, he'd tell him, but not tonight.

CHAPTER FOUR

Greg lifted his foot and kicked a rock across the sidewalk. It flew down the street and rattled into the gutter. He wasn't sure if he wanted to get home and hear about the surprise. What if his parents planned on moving? He'd have to make new friends. What if the kids in a new school didn't like him? Would he ever find another best friend like Tommy?

Darn, it didn't seem fair. He'd just got his bedroom all fixed up. Lightweight gliders hung from the ceiling and his model airplanes lined the shelves. He had his favorite cartoon drawings tacked to the walls and his mom had even framed a couple of them.

Greg plodded through the yard and opened the back door.

"Hi, Mom."

"In here, honey."

Greg stepped up the three steps from the back door into the kitchen area. "Awesome, it smells great. Did you bake chocolate brownies?" Before his mom answered, he'd spotted a plate with two layers of brownies on the cupboard. He reached.

"No more than one," warned his mom. "How was school?"

"Okay." Greg munched the brownie. He didn't feel like talking about his trouble with the Barbarian.

"Your dad should be home in half an hour and we'll leave. Get changed into good slacks and a dress shirt."

Greg pulled his face. "Do I have to? Can't I wear my jeans?"

"No, the Toreador is a nice restaurant and you're to dress accordingly."

"But nobody'll look at me."

His mom frowned. "I will."

"Ah, Mom." He finished eating and left the kitchen. There was no point in arguing, she wouldn't change her mind.

By six o'clock everyone was dressed and ready. At the back door Greg tied the laces on his runners.

"Where are your dress shoes, young man?"

He looked up. His mom stood three steps above at the entrance to the kitchen. "I like my runners."

"They're scuffed and dirty. And while you're at it change your socks. Black, please."

"Nobody sees my socks," Greg grumbled.

"Do it."

Seeing there was no point in arguing anymore, he strolled to his bedroom. He pulled off his white socks and noticed they were a little dirty on the bottom. He rolled one sock in a ball and tossed it at the small basketball hoop on the back of his door. All right, a three-point shot! He dribbled down the basketball court, and the crowd went wild, cheering him on.

"Go, Greg, go. G-R-E-G-!"

He realized his mom was calling and not cheering fans. "Greg, hurry up. We're leaving now."

"Coming." Shoes in his hand, he scurried to the kitchen and leaped over the three steps to the landing at the back door. He shoved his feet into his black loafers. His mom wasn't nearby and he noticed she'd left the key in the deadbolt so he locked the door, dashed through the yard and scrambled into the back seat of the car.

His dad turned, "Ready, partner?"

When they arrived at the restaurant, the man at the front desk smiled and said, "Good evening Mr. and Mrs. Hutchins." He nodded at Greg. "Your table is ready."

Following directly behind the man, Greg noticed the man's suit wiggled like a penguin. Moving his bum from side to side, Greg waddled and copied the penguin walk.

"Enough." His father whispered in his ear.

Greg felt a hand on his shoulder and he straightened.

Seated on one side of the booth opposite his parents, he peered at the plants hanging from the ceiling with their long trailing vines. It reminded him of a jungle and he pretended he was Greg, King of the Jungle, sitting on his royal throne and all the people were his subjects.

His daydream was interrupted when the penguin man handed him a menu, but he didn't need one. He knew what he wanted. Pizza. A medium-sized number ten with lots of pineapple, bacon, and extra cheese.

The waitress arrived at the table and flipped open a little notebook. "Would you like to order now?"

Greg noticed her white blouse, black skirt and black shoes. Black and white. Great for penguins. Boring for people.

With all the plants Greg figured the restaurant should have a different name. He'd call it The Jungle Beat. When hungry customers came in, they'd hear the beating of tom-tom drums and the screeching of wild birds with orange, yellow and green parrots perched in trees. On the wall there'd be masks of different tribes with gruesome faces. He imagined servers dressed in grass outfits and carrying spears.

"Have you decided?" The voice came out of nowhere but Greg already knew what he wanted.

He gave his order and the waitress winked. "Right." "And you ma'am?" she asked Greg's mom."

Greg watched his parents and wondered when they'll spill the beans about moving. They'd be surprised that he'd already guessed.

In no time the girl came back with their salads. His parents speared their lettuce and chewed slowly. He squirmed, anxious for them to tell him the news.

Finally, after his parents must have chewed every piece of lettuce to mush, his dad put down his fork. “Your mother and I have an exciting announcement. It will mean some changes in the house but I think we can accommodate everyone.”

“Who’s coming?”

They both grinned and his mother said, “Well, it might even happen on my birthday.” She beamed at his dad and back at Greg as she clasped her hands. “How lovely. Babies born on the same day as me.”

“Whose baby?” asked Greg. He had a funny feeling in his stomach.

“Ours,” they said together. The grins on their faces reached from ear to ear.

“Oh no,” muttered Greg.

“Yes,” replied his mom.

“Your mother had the pregnancy confirmed and we wanted to celebrate,” said his dad. “Now you’ll have a brother or sister, or perhaps even both.

“Darn, who wants them anyway?” Greg pouted.

“We do,” they both responded. Their smiles weren’t so big now though, instead they appeared to be worried.

Greg leaned forward. “Why do you need another kid? Aren’t I enough?”

“Now Greg. We love you very much, but your mother and I always wanted more children. We’ll be twice blessed.”

But Greg didn't think it was any blessing with a baby brother or sister crying at night, getting into his room and touching his stuff.

"Don't you like our family the way it is?" Greg stared at his father. They hadn't even asked him what he thought.

"Won't the newspaper announcement about the twins be exciting?" said his mom.

"Twins!" Greg's mouth dropped open and he gasped for a breath. He hadn't heard right.

His mom nodded, her eyes sparkling "Right, twins. Two bundles of joy."

"We wanted you to know first," said his dad. "There'll be a lot of activity at the house, preparing for two babies. Double the fun and pleasure."

Double the trouble. If he didn't already have enough problems with the Barbarian, now Double Trouble was on the way.

CHAPTER FIVE

Greg woke up on Monday morning knowing it was going to be the most miserable day of his life. Last night he'd dreamed about the Barbarian, twin Barbarians, one on each side of him, with plastic lunch kits. They shook them like baby rattles and screamed in his ears. "I'm going to get you. You'll have Double Trouble."

At school he couldn't eat outside because it was raining. The morning passed in a blur and at noon his heart pounded faster when the bell rang indicating it was time to go to the dreaded lunchroom. What would he do? When he stepped outside the classroom he spotted Tommy in the hall.

"So what's the surprise? Come on, tell me," urged Tommy.

Greg kept on walking down the hall and mumbled under his breath, "Mom's having a baby."

"A baby? Wow! Great!" Tommy jumped up and punched the air. When Greg didn't answer, Tommy said, "I'd love a baby brother or sister."

"How about two?"

Tommy's face brightened and his eyes were wide. He stopped and gawked at Greg. "Two? You mean not one baby, but two? Twins?"

"Yeah, you catch on real fast."

"Great," shouted Tommy. "This is totally awesome. We'll be able to walk them every day."

"Listen, Tommy, we're not talking about dogs."

"I know, but babies are a lot of fun. Way more fun than dogs. You can teach them to talk."

"Yeah and how about teaching them to be quiet?" Greg was getting tired of Tommy's enthusiasm. "Too bad it's not your mom who's going to have twins."

For a few minutes he'd forgotten all about the Barbarian but when they got closer to the lunchroom, Tommy said in a low voice, "The Barbarian's here. I saw him during a class change. Boy, did he look mad."

Greg shivered at the idea of sitting next to him.

"What're you going to do?" asked Tommy.

"Just eat my lunch and hope he forgets about me."

Changing the subject, Tommy said, "Look, there's the Dungeon Master."

"You'd better not let her hear you," Greg whispered.

Mrs. Bostock, the supervisor, guarded the entrance with her arms folded across her chest, her feet planted firmly apart and a scowl on her face that said to Greg, *Mess with me and you're dead meat.*

Feeling her cold glare, Greg hurried and headed for his assigned seat. Tommy took his place at another table.

Sitting next to the Barbarian, Greg pretended to ignore him but out of the corner of his eyes he watched the Barbarian open his plastic lunch box. He pulled out a sandwich and quickly stuffed it in his mouth.

Greg glanced away, trying to forget the guy. Peering into his lunch bag, he spotted a can of pop. He pulled back the tab and the pop fizzled. He guzzled three large mouthfuls and started to open his pudding when he burped. Not one burp, but two loud belches.

Heads jerked up and everyone at the table gawked at the Barbarian, thinking he'd done it.

"Do it again," a boy jeered.

"Hey, Barbarian, you been practising?" said another student.

"More, more," kids chanted.

The word spread and soon the entire lunchroom pointed and laughed at the Barbarian.

"Let's hear you. This time louder," someone said.

While another kid shouted, "Can you bring that up again and we'll vote on it?"

The Barbarian's face got redder and Greg felt sorry for him, but it was funny with all the kids giggling, and he laughed too.

Plop.

Something wet and slimy hit his cheek. The warm sloppy mess slithered down his face and Greg tore at his skin. He squeezed a squishy greenish-black ball.

Greg turned and faced the Barbarian who wore a satisfied smirk.

"How does it feel, shrimp?"

"Is this what your mom feeds you?" Greg shot back. "No wonder you're so weird."

"Everyone settle down." Mrs. Bostock's voice boomed above the noise.

"He threw..." Greg tried to explain, but Bossy's grip on his collar tightened as she dragged him out of his seat.

"He started it," sputtered the Barbarian who was being hauled out of the room at the same time.

Out in the hall, Mrs. Bostock glared at them. "You like making a mess, so now the two of you can clean up."

Greg stammered, "But, but..."

"I'm not interested in any of your lame excuses, young man."

The other students filed out of the lunchroom, snickering at Greg and the Barbarian.

"Good shot." One boy gave Greg a thumbs-up as he walked by.

Another said, "Hey, Greg, did you like the salad?"

A fierce look from Mrs. Bostock silenced them and the students moved away quickly.

She tapped Greg on the shoulder. "Eyes front. March."

He trudged down the hall not daring to look at the Barbarian who kept in step beside him. In the caretaker's room they were each handed a mop and a bucket and told to fill it with water.

Back in the lunchroom, Mrs. Bostock said, "Fred, you start at the back and scrub all the tables, then do the floor. Greg, you start at the front and do the same thing."

The water was hot and slippery with a strong smell just like at home when his mom cleaned. After wringing out the cloth, Greg washed the table tops.

Puddles of spilt juice and pop formed sticky pools along with breadcrumbs littering the surfaces. Usually each group tidied their own space, but today they got a holiday, thanks to the Barbarian.

Taking a quick look, Greg tried to spot Mrs. Bostock but she was nowhere in sight so he wiped the floor until he heard a shuffle behind him.

"Think you're smart, don't you, shrimp?" The Barbarian loomed above him.

Greg stuck out his chin and said, "Yes, I am. Thank you very much."

"Well, try this."

The smell of soapy water itched his nose as the Barbarian pushed the rag towards Greg's face. He twisted his head and squirmed to get away, but the Barbarian clutched him around the chest.

"Still think you're so smart?"

Before Greg had chance to reply, the Barbarian loosened his grip and Greg stumbled forward.

"La, la, lalala, laaa." Singing came from the hall.

Wiping his chin with his sleeve, Greg bent down and continued scrubbing.

"Hi, Greg." Miss Clark stood in the open doorway. "I see you're giving Mrs. Bostock extra help."

He rubbed his hands on his jeans.

"I wanted to mention something to you." She stepped into the room. "I know you have an interest in drawing and I've been thinking you might like to prepare a portfolio."

Greg stared back, not having a clue what she meant.

Miss Clark continued. "Collect all your best cartoons and put them in a large folder, and voila," she raised her hands, "you'll have a portfolio." She paused and studied Greg. When he didn't answer she eyed the Barbarian. "Hello, Fred. Why don't you do the same?"

The Barbarian beamed and Greg wondered why he looked so pleased. Probably nobody ever said anything nice to him.

Not wanting Miss Clark to forget him, Greg burst in, "Sure, Miss Clark, I'll do it."

"Fine. Start working on it, Greg, and if you have any questions, feel free to ask me. You too, Fred."

She started for the door and turned. "The water's for washing the floor, Fred." She winked at him.

The Barbarian's face turned red. "Yes, Miss Clark."

A few seconds later Bossy's heavy footsteps echoed in the hall and she thumped into the room. After inspecting everything she said, "These are satisfactory. Before you go out dump the water in the caretaker's sink and hang the cloths to dry."

Greg nodded.

Mrs. Bostock pointed at him. "And tomorrow, you'll be moved to a new table."

Greg wanted to jump and shout, but he didn't want her to know how relieved he was to be moved away from the Barbarian so he quietly said, "Okay."

She shook her finger at them. "Remember, from now on I'll be watching both of you and your behavior had better improve."

The Barbarian nodded and Greg replied, "It will." He didn't tell her that once he was away from the Barbarian; his whole life was going to improve.

CHAPTER SIX

At home that night, Greg worked on his art. Mr. Dickinson, the school principal, had announced a contest. Any student could submit a portfolio of four to five original drawings or paintings. The best entry from each school would be sent to a panel of artists and the city-wide winner received a gift certificate for art supplies.

Sitting at his desk, Greg pulled out a pencil, a piece of paper and drew a circle.

He eyed it, thinking about what he'd do next. "Looks like a billiard ball," he said. "I wonder what I can do to it?" He drew two large eyes, a nose and a mouth. "Okay, now for a hat and vest. You're on a mission from another planet and no one knows the pool cue you're holding is really your secret communicator." Greg drew a cue in the little creature's hand.

"With this you can talk to your space craft."

He drew an oval shape in the background. "Here's the ship that transported you to earth from your home planet. I'm going to call you Eight Ball the Alien."

On the bottom of the page he wrote the title.

"Greg. It's time for bed," his mom called from the kitchen.

"All right." After putting the drawing in a folder, he changed into his flannelette pajamas. In half an hour he was in bed and dreaming of walking through an art store where he saw all the wonderful supplies he'd buy. Racks with huge rolls of fluorescent pink, green and orange drawing paper caught his attention. They floated off the rolls and twisted up into the air and swooped down in the shape of a dragon. Orange flames shot from the mouth and singed his skin.

"No, no," Greg screamed. Cracking and hissing flames surrounded him. Sweat poured down his face. He waved his arms and screamed, "Help me!"

"Greg, wake up. You're dreaming," said a voice.

He couldn't move and horrible heat suffocated him.

"Come on; roll yourself out of the blankets. Here, like this."

Greg opened his eyes and saw his mom pulling on the covers. He tried to wiggle out of them.

"You've wrapped yourself like an Egyptian mummy."

"There was a dragon, Mom."

"Ssh, honey, it's okay. You were dreaming."

Greg rubbed his forehead. It felt as if he'd been singed. Lying in his bed, he recalled the creature spouting fire, destroying everything in its path and burning all his cartoons. It all seemed so real.

* * *

First period the next morning was math. Mr. Peabody walked around the room while the students worked. He bent over Greg's desk. "Good. I see you're finished. How'd you like to help Angela?"

"Sure." Greg went to her desk. She raised her head and smiled. Angela was the nicest girl in the whole school, never mean and even if she didn't have the best marks, she did okay. Greg knew because he always listened when Mr. Peabody asked the students for their mark on an exercise or test.

"Need help, Angela?"

She nodded. "I can't figure out how to calculate the area in this question."

"I'll show you." Greg drew two rectangles, one inside the other. "I multiply and after I subtract and the difference is the area."

"You make it look so easy when you draw a picture. Thanks."

Greg replied, "No problem." He enjoyed helping others, especially Angela. On the way back to his seat, he hummed.

"Ssh." Mr. Peabody gave him a stern look.

"Oops." Greg grinned. So far things were going pretty good today.

The next period Greg went to the library to get a free reading book and headed for the tall stacks in the corner. Paper rustled and he peered around the edge of the big brown book case. To his surprise the Barbarian sat hunched on the carpet with his shoes off and reading a book with a bright blue cover.

The Barbarian glared. "You tell anyone about this and you'll be dead meat." Glowering at Greg, he hugged the book to his chest and tried to hide it with his hands. "Go away, shrimp."

"Okay, okay. I'm gone." Greg stepped back. How could he tell anyone anything when he didn't even see the title? Besides, he didn't want the Barbarian looking for another fight, but he couldn't help wondering. What was the Barbarian reading and why the big secret over a book?

Wow, no wonder all the kids thought the guy was weird.

CHAPTER SEVEN

It was 7:30 in the morning and Greg chewed the end of his pencil. He'd finished 'Eight Ball the Alien'. Now he doodled and sketched a boy. His belly bulged and his tongue flopped out the side of his mouth. For fun Greg added a club in the cartoon character's left hand.

"You remind me of a caveman just like the Barbarian. And that's what I'm going to call you." He scribbled, 'The Barbarian', at the bottom of the page.

He peered at the clock and saw it was quarter to eight, time to get ready for school. After dressing and eating, he stuffed his loose-leaf and books into his backpack.

"I'll only show you to Tommy," he said as he put the caveman-Barbarian sketch in his notebook. "You won't go into the contest, and nobody else will ever see you."

"Bye, Mom," Greg yelled as he darted out the door and headed for school.

After homeroom check in, Greg hurried to his language arts class. When he opened his binder papers fell out.

"Please hand in your writing assignment," said Mr. Millar as the students settled in their desks.

After rummaging through his papers and dropping some on the floor, Greg finally found his homework and he picked up the scattered sheets.

"Good likeness," said Jason Holbert.

Greg wondered what he was talking about so he turned to check. Jason was a new boy who'd moved into the school last week. Bigger than most of the other kids, he didn't say much, just watched and Greg had the feeling he secretly laughed at the other kids.

Jason and Chris peered at a piece of paper.

"Looks like a caveman." Jason scoffed.

"Yeah, he should have called him Neanderthal man," replied Chris and he stuck his tongue out the side of his mouth and crossed his eyes.

Jason snickered.

Stretching, Greg tried to see what was so funny. He couldn't figure it out until Chris held up the cartoon drawing of the Barbarian and said, "Hey Greg, we like your picture."

"That's mine, give it back."

"Don't you want the Barbarian to see it?" Chris smirked and dangled the paper out of Greg's reach.

"Come on, it's mine." Greg stretched, trying to grab the sheet.

Chris pulled back. "This is good. Don't you think so, Jason?"

Jason didn't say anything. He calmly took the paper, folded it and put it in his back pocket. Ignoring both of them, Jason straightened and paid attention to the teacher.

Greg groaned. He knew there was no way he'd ever get the picture back. Darn, why'd he ever bring it to school? What if Jason showed it to the Barbarian? He'd be dead before the end of the day.

For the rest of the period, Greg sneaked peeks at Jason who seemed to have forgotten all about the sketch. Good. He didn't need to worry.

However, by lunchtime, Greg discovered he wasn't going to get off so easy. As he made his way down the hall, Frank came over. "You really nailed the Barbarian this time."

Before Greg could answer, another student said, "Nice art work. Looks like the Barbarian. I wonder what he'll think."

By the time Greg reached Tommy's room, his palms were sweaty and he'd decided he wouldn't be eating inside. He couldn't face the Barbarian.

Tommy came out of his classroom and said, "I've heard stories about your drawing all morning. Why'd you do it?" He frowned.

"I drew a picture and I wanted you to see it, no one else, but Chris and Jason got hold of it."

"Good thing the Barbarian isn't here today or you'd really be in big trouble."

"He's away?" asked Greg hopefully.

Tommy nodded. "Yeah, I didn't see him, so you don't have to worry."

Greg took two big gulps of air and his breathing slowed down. Today might be okay after all.

"Come on," I'm hungry."

"So am I," said Greg. His appetite had returned.

After a quiet lunch with no signs of the Barbarian, the 1:30 bell rang and Greg hurried down the hall thankful Jason and Chris weren't in his math class.

"We'll be working in groups today so you can move your desks," said Mr. Peabody.

Greg checked for Angela. He'd get in the same group as her.

"Angela," he called.

She didn't seem to hear him so he said it a little louder. "Angela."

This time she turned and he gave his friendliest smile, expecting one back. She stared, her eyes cold, as if she didn't even know him.

He ignored her strange look, pulled his desk close to hers and said, "Let's work together."

She clamped her mouth shut and ignored him the whole time, until class finished. As they lined up, Greg started… "Math seems easier now, doesn't it?"

Angela glared at him. "How could you?"

"Uh, I…"

"Why are you so mean to Fred?" Her eyes blazed.

"But, but...," Greg stammered.

Before he finished Angela said, "Your drawing of Fred was awful. I always believed you were a nice person."

Greg's mouth hung open as she marched away. She hadn't even given him a chance to explain. If only he could tell her that he'd never meant for anyone to see the picture except Tommy. With his shoulders slumped, he walked down the hall. Alone.

When the bell rang to go home, Greg was the glad the school day was over. He signed out a book from the library and by the time he got outside there weren't any other kids. As he rounded the corner of the school, the Barbarian loomed in front of him, blocking the sun.

"Thought you'd never come out."

"But...but...you're sick," said Greg.

"Might have been healthier for you if I was." The Barbarian put his hands on Greg's chest and pushed.

Greg tried to dodge and make a run for it, but each time the Barbarian moved in front of him "You're not going anywhere." His huge body barred the way.

Greg's heart hammered and he glanced around the schoolyard.

"See anybody to help you?" The Barbarian looked from side to side. "I don't." He pushed Greg's chest again, crushing him against the cement wall.

"N...n...no," stuttered Greg. He hated it when he got scared and started to stutter, but he couldn't help it.

"You know what, shrimp?" The Barbarian's breath heated Greg's face. "I don't like your drawings." With his big meaty hands he pinned Greg's shoulders.

"A…a…all I was…" Greg stammered, but he didn't have time to finish because a grating noise came from a nearby window.

Suddenly it opened and Miss Clark poked her head out and said, "Fred, come inside, please?"

The Barbarian stopped pushing, dropped his hands, appearing surprised and said, "Sure."

As Greg started to back away, the Barbarian snarled and muttered, "I'm not finished with you yet."

Greg took a big breath and scrambled out of the schoolyard. The darned picture had caused him nothing but trouble. He shivered and wondered if there was more to come.

***

Fred yanked on the school door and stepped inside. He stomped into Miss Clark's room. Why'd she want to talk to him anyway? He'd almost got the shrimp and he deserved a fat lip. Fred's neck and face were hot and he clenched his fists.

"Hello, Fred." Miss Clark smiled. "Please sit down, so we can talk."

Fred didn't say anything. He jerked out a chair, sat and rested his elbows on the table.

Miss Clark picked up a file from her desk and sat across from him. She opened the folder. "I really like your art ideas."

"Mm." Fred didn't feel like talking about art.

Miss Clark continued, "Have you considered what I asked you the other day in the lunchroom?"

Fred hunched his shoulders.

"You have superior drawing skills and I'd like you to complete a portfolio for the contest."

"Why? Greg's better."

She shook her head. "No, not better, but different."

"All the kids like his art."

"I know. His cartoons are cute and funny."

"Yeah, like the one of me."

Miss Clark frowned. "You know. I don't really believe Greg meant to hurt you."

"Huh." Fred snorted. "I think he did."

"Try to forget Greg."

"I can't." The anger boiled in Fred. When he'd come to school after lunch the kids had laughed and the minute Jason showed him the picture, he decided he'd get even with the shrimp. "The whole school saw Greg's drawing and I'm gonna punch his lights out. Teach him a lesson."

Miss Clark shook her head. "No. It will only get you in trouble."

"Yeah, it'll be worth it."

“Think about what would happen to you if you did anything to Greg. You’re an intelligent young man. Please don’t give in to your desire to get even.”

Fred stared at the floor and clenched his hands.

Miss Clark leaned across the table and put her hand under his chin, making him look at her. “Promise me you won’t do anything foolish, Fred. Do it for yourself and for me. I have great faith in you. Now show me the best side of yourself. Okay?”

“Well, I’ll try,” he mumbled.

“Think about all your fine qualities, Fred. You’re a good person and I’d love to see more of your art. Why don’t you go home and get to work on it?”

“Yeah.” He shuffled out of the room. Right now he couldn’t promise, but he’d think about it anyway.

CHAPTER EIGHT

After supper Greg sat at the desk in his bedroom, thinking about new cartoon ideas. The blank white paper in front of him seemed overpowering. How would he ever win the art contest?

Sketching, erasing, and trying again, Greg finally drew a clown face and body. He added a loose-fitting outfit and big shoes with turned-up toes. Beside the clown he drew a tiny dog with a polka-dot jacket. In the background he filled in a large tent and added an elephant.

"Greg, fifteen minutes till bed time," his mom called from the kitchen.

After he put his pencils away, he left the drawing on his desk for his mom to see while he changed into his pajamas. He'd just snuggled under the covers when she tapped on the door.

"Come in," he called.

His mom entered and peered at his desk. She picked up the drawing. "This is good. There's lots of detail on the clown and the dog's cute."

Sitting on the edge of the bed, she studied him. "How'd school go today?"

"Okay." He couldn't face his mom's stare so he looked at the wall behind her. After a long silence he said, "Not so good, I guess."

"Problems with another student?"

"Kinda." Greg clutched the corner of a blanket.

"Well …" He hesitated. "I drew a picture to show Tommy."

"A picture of what?" His mom wasn't going to let him get away easy.

"The Barbarian." Greg paused, hoping his mom didn't ask any more questions.

She frowned. "The boy you told me about last week?"

"Uh-huh. His real name's Fred, but everyone calls him the Barbarian. Nobody likes him because he's a bully."

"What was the picture like?"

"Well … uh." He paused, not really wanting to admit to his mom how the Barbarian appeared in the drawing. "Well, he …" Greg tried to think of what to say. "He was kinda fatter in the picture."

"Really?"

"I put a …" Greg hesitated, feeling kind of bad that he'd given the Barbarian a big belly, way larger than he really had. "I put a … a big stomach on him."

His mom raised her eyebrows. "Oh. Anything else?"

"Yeah." Greg hung his head. The more he thought about the drawing, the meaner it seemed. "I gave him a big nose."

Tell the truth thought Greg. “And I gave him a big stick.”

His mom’s jaw dropped. “Did Fred see the picture?”

“Yeah. The whole school saw it.”

Her face clouded over. “Oh, Greg, it wasn’t very nice to show everybody.”

After Greg told his mom about Chris and Jason, she said, “Do you realize how much this must have hurt Fred?”

Not much, he figured. The guy sure didn’t have any feelings when he pounded on other kids. “But the Barbarian’s a big bully.”

“Perhaps he is, but you mustn’t provoke him.”

“Me!” His mom really didn’t realize how scared he’d been when the Barbarian had caught him after school. He shivered. “I hate him, mom. He’s big, mean and ugly.”

“Then leave him alone.”

“How can I? He picks on me.”

“I know. This boy may be everything you say but he has feelings like everybody else.”

“No, he doesn’t,” Greg protested.

“He’s still a person who wants to be liked by the other students.”

“He doesn’t care about friends. He doesn’t have any.”

“Perhaps he pretends not to care because he hurts inside.”

“What about when he pushes me? That hurts.”

“I know, but has he ever hit you?”

Greg thought about it. The Barbarian had shoved him a couple of times, but never hit him.

His mom walked towards the door. "You have your dad or me to talk to anytime about your problems."

"But Mom, you should see him. His hair's really a mess and he always looks so wild." Greg sat up and ran his hands through his hair to make it stick out like the Barbarian's.

"Well, we can't always judge people by how they look. There could be problems in his family. We don't really know, so give him a chance. Don't antagonize him so he wants to fight with you. Okay?"

Reluctantly, Greg agreed. "Okay, I'll try." He wasn't sure if it would work though, especially if the other person didn't know that he, too, was supposed to be trying.

CHAPTER NINE

The next day Greg was convinced that everyone at school had forgotten the Barbarian drawing. Nobody said anything about it all morning and he crossed his fingers hoping he was right.

At noon, Tommy's class had been dismissed early so he was eating when Greg entered the lunchroom. Greg sat in his new seat, in the corner, far away from the enemy. If only the Barbarian was willing to forget the drawing, then so was he.

"Ask to go to the bathroom," Tommy whispered as he quickly moved by.

Bathroom? What'd Tommy mean? Greg spotted his friend heading out the door so he asked to be excused and scurried down the hall and into the boys' bathroom.

"Look at this." Tommy pointed. "I thought I'd better show you."

Greg gasped when he saw the large, sloppy printing pencilled on the wall. It read, 'Greg's art stinks'. Under it was a stick drawing of a boy with little tight curls. Greg touched the back of his neck where his hair curled a little.

"Let's try rubbing it out before anyone sees it. I'll get an eraser from my desk."

Tommy left and Greg gawked at the jagged letters. Why couldn't the Barbarian let him forget?

In a flash Tommy came back. "I've got two erasers," he said, handing one to Greg. After a few minutes of steady rubbing Tommy said, "Don't worry, we'll be finished soon and nobody will ever know it was ever here." He stopped and stepped back. "Who do you think did it?"

"The Barbarian. Who else?" replied Greg.

Tommy shook his head. "I don't know. Do you really think he wants everyone to know about your drawing? Doesn't make sense to me."

"The Barbarian never makes sense and he's never going to let me forget. Miss Clark stopped him from pounding me so he probably decided to get even."

Frowning, Tommy said, "Seems to me I'd want to forget."

"The Barbarian's not after you. He's out to get me."

Tommy pulled his face. "But it's strange. Why this?" He pointed to the wall.

"Cause he's an A-1 jerk." Greg rubbed harder on the pencil lines.

Tommy shrugged. "Maybe, but I don't think so."

"Done," exclaimed Greg as he erased the last part of the figure and backed away to check his work. He put his hand to his forehead. "It looks worse. I rubbed the paint right off and look at the holes I've made." He ran his hand over the gouges in the wall.

"Okay boys, you'd better come with me," a harsh voice sounded from the doorway.

Greg whirled and faced the school principal who had his arms crossed and a scowl on his face. "Let's go." He ushered them down the hall.

In a few minutes they were in front of the principal's big office desk. Greg shifted from one foot to the other while beside him Tommy stood very still.

Mr. Dickinson sat down and studied them. His gaze rested on Greg. "What happened?"

Greg wasn't sure if he should tell the principal about his drawing of the Barbarian. It'd probably get him into more trouble, but what if he didn't tell and somebody else did? It'd be worse for him. He took a gulp of air and figured he'd better tell the whole story.

The principal listened and when Greg finished he asked a few questions and said, "You are dismissed, Tommy."

Greg shifted. He was glad Tommy didn't have to stay because none of this was his fault. He'd only tried to help.

Mr. Dickinson jotted a few notes on a piece of paper while Greg squinted and wished he could read the small up-side-down writing. After a few minutes the principal put down his pen and said, "I'll be talking to Fred and after I've heard his story, I'll discuss this matter with you again. And there will be consequences."

Greg gasped. Consequences. He hated the word. What would happen to him and the Barbarian?

CHAPTER TEN

Fred dropped the empty pop can onto the sidewalk, stomped on it and then raised his right foot and kicked as hard as he could, sending the can clanking down the street.

His eyes stung but he kept on walking, refusing to cry. Thanks to Greg he'd been accused of something he didn't do. Mr. Dickinson had told him Greg's story and he'd said he didn't do it. He'd never even seen the writing or the drawing on the bathroom wall, but nobody believed him.

If only he could get away from this school. If only he could live with his mom. Fred swallowed and tried to make the lump in his throat go down. He wanted to run, run away somewhere. Anywhere. But where would he go?

Miss Clark's voice echoed in his head and he heard her saying, 'Fred, work on all the things you can do well. Remember, you have your own special, good qualities. Let your better part show'. Her voice faded and her last words echoed over and over. 'Forget Greg, forget…'

But how could he? The shrimp had blamed it all on him.

Fred gazed at the other houses in the neighborhood. He lived in the oldest one with fading and peeling paint. He wished his father had rented a nicer house and he'd bring someone home. A friend? He snorted. "Ha." He didn't have any friends, so who cared where he lived?

Once inside he pulled a package of four meat patties from the freezer. He wouldn't tell his dad about what happened at school. His dad was crabby enough lately without hearing about more problems.

It wasn't long before the screen door squeaked and banged. "Hi, Dad," called Fred. As his dad came into the kitchen, Fred noticed his glum look.

His dad seemed to realize that Fred had spoken and mumbled, "Oh, hi."

Something was bothering his dad and maybe he'd tell Fred.

"Supper ready yet?" His dad plopped into the chair.

"Yup, almost. All I have to do is get a can of beans and the buns."

Before his dad answered, the phone rang and Mr. Farley picked it up. "Yes, Mr. Dickinson, this is Fred's father." The scowl on his face grew bigger and his voice got quieter.

Straining to hear, Fred slowly opened the fridge and lifted out the package of buns, trying not to let the cover crackle.

Stealing a sideways glance, he saw his dad close his fist and his knuckles turn white.

"I see," said his dad.

Fred doubted he understood anything about the shrimp and the trouble he caused.

After a long pause his dad continued. "No, I didn't hear a word about it. Yes, it certainly will be discussed with him." His dad hung up and the lines in his forehead deepened.

"Son, you've got a lot of explaining to do."

Fred pressed his fist on his stomach. It always ached when he got upset. The lump in his throat choked him. How could he make his dad understand about the shrimp and the caveman drawing?

His dad drummed his fingers on the kitchen table. "Let's hear it."

"Um, well, a kid at school always bugs me." He twiddled his thumbs and stared down, not wanting to look his father in the eye.

"Who's this kid?"

"Greg Hutchins."

"What's he done to you?"

After taking a deep breath, Fred said, "He drew a picture of me and..."

"What'd you do to him that the principal has to phone?"

Fred decided he'd better tell his dad the truth because he'd find out anyways. He raised his head and said, "I was going to beat him up."

His dad's lips twisted and his mouth pulled down and Fred worried about telling the truth, but outside the school he'd been ready to pound Greg until Miss Clark called him and it was good she did. She saved him from getting into more trouble and the shrimp wasn't worth it.

"Can't you keep out of trouble? I've got enough problems without getting calls from the school."

"Yeah, Dad." There was no point in trying to explain things to his dad. He never listened. He lectured.

"No more calls from the school." His father waved his finger. "You hear me."

Fred nodded.

The meal continued in silence. Cold hamburgers and beans were hard to swallow and he'd lost his appetite.

His father wolfed down his supper. When he finished he said, "You can do the dishes. I have to go back to work."

Fred would have liked to know why, but he didn't ask.

"I'll be home late. You be in bed."

In a few minutes the back door clicked and Fred was alone. He cleared the table, rinsed the plates and scrubbed the fry pan and pot. All the time he worked he wondered if Greg's parents got a call. He hoped so. Teach the shrimp a lesson.

At bedtime he undressed, put on his pajamas and crawled under the covers, trying not to think about school and how much he missed his mom.

Later a car door slammed and a key jingled in the lock. Rolling on his side, he tried to sleep. His father talked to someone on the phone and he could make out some of the words. Principal…trouble school.

Fred clenched the sheets and listened harder, but his dad's voice was too low to hear anything else. It couldn't be the principal. He wouldn't phone this late. So who was his dad talking to?

Feeling tired and alone, he punched his pillow and then curled into a ball. The ache in his stomach wouldn't go away.

CHAPTER ELEVEN

After school Fred reported to Mr. Dickinson's office. As he walked in, he spotted Greg sitting in one of the chairs in front of the principal's desk.

"Sit down, Fred," ordered Mr. Dickinson.

Fred didn't like the tone of his voice. The principal used it on other students when they were in trouble. Sinking into the chair, he watched Greg out of the corner of his eye. The shrimp sat really straight and so still, like he was frozen to the spot. Good. Teach him a lesson. The shrimp deserved to be scared. He'd finally pay for all the trouble he'd caused.

The principal glared at Fred and Greg. "The two of you have denied any involvement with writing in the bathroom. However, both of you have behaved very badly, so I'm giving you a project to do together after school."

Greg gasped and dropped back in his chair like he'd been shot.

"There will be no arguing, fighting or complaining." Mr. Dickinson eyed Greg. "Do I make myself clear?"

The shrimp's eyes were wide open, like he'd seen a ghost. His head bobbed up and down and he mumbled, "Yes."

Enjoying the shrimp's uneasiness, Fred smiled to himself.

The principal glared at him. "And you?"

He sat tall. "Yes, sir. I understand."

"What do we have to do?" Greg whined.

"Listen and I'll explain," said the principal. "The both of you will sand and paint the defaced wall in the boys' bathroom."

"Paint?" Greg moaned. "It'll take hours."

"You should have considered that when you were busy making the gouges."

"What about Tommy?" asked Greg.

"I believe it is you two who've been arguing and causing the trouble. Therefore, you'll do the repair work. I've talked to your parents and they all agree that this action is suitable."

Fred grinned. The shrimp wasn't going to get out of this.

* * *

Working with the Barbarian! Greg could hardly believe his ears. His lower lip quivered. His parents hadn't said anything to him. When had Mr. Dickinson phoned? He hoped the Barbarian got in big trouble at home. Serve him right.

"The bathroom will be closed until you two have finished your job."

Greg groaned. "When do we have to start?"

"Right now." Mr. Dickinson pulled out two old shirts from a box on the side cupboard and handed one to each of them. "Put it on to protect your clothes."

The shirt hung down to Greg's knees and he had to roll up the sleeves so his hands stuck out.

"Here's the sandpaper. Let's get you two started."

When they reached the bathroom at the end of the hall, Greg noticed the closed door with a large sign attached to it.

BOYS

USE THE BATHROOM BY ROOM TEN

Mr. Dickinson opened the door and flicked on the lights. Pointing to the wall to the right of the sinks, he said, "Fred, you can sand those spots, but press lightly."

To his horror, Greg noticed there were two more places where the message, 'Greg's art stinks', had been written, below and to the left of the two sinks. The spots where he and Tommy had erased were brown smears on the chipped and gouged grey wall.

Mr. Dickinson picked up a small white pail from the corner and pried open the plastic top. "This is called 'mud'. It's a patching compound and Greg, you can fill all the holes you made. Use a little at a time. Here, try it." He handed Greg a small broad knife.

Greg dug out some of the thick white stuff and pressed it into the gouge. He'd seen his dad using something like this. He pulled the knife along the surface, making it smooth.

"That's the idea," said Mr. Dickinson. "This mud is quick drying."

The boys filled more holes and Mr. Dickinson checked their work and ran his fingers along the wall. "Good. When you paint this wall, the repaired parts won't show. In fact, I think a quick coat of paint on the spots tomorrow before school, will ensure a good job. Now, you're both finished for tonight. We can leave the supplies here."

Greg took off his paint shirt and hung it over a partition, and followed the Barbarian and the principal out of the bathroom.

"See you tomorrow morning, one hour before bell time. I'll meet the two of you at the front door." The principal turned left while Greg turned right and ran to the nearest exit door. No way did he want to be caught by the Barbarian.

Fred followed the principal down the hall until Mr. Dickinson went into the office.

"Goodnight, Fred."

"Night," mumbled Fred. Free at last. It was almost supper time and he walked fast, hoping his father wouldn't be home yet. But as he neared the house he spotted the car parked on the front street. Opening the back door he called, "Hi, Dad." Would his dad be in a bad mood because supper wasn't ready?

Mr. Farley stood at the stove stirring something in a pot. "Hello, son."

Fred entered the kitchen. "Can I help?"

"Wash your hands first."

"Sure, Dad." Fred twisted the tap, squirted soap on his palm and plunged his hands under the warm water.

"How was school today?"

"Oh, fine." Fred wasn't sure if his dad knew exactly what he'd been doing but if he didn't know he wouldn't tell him, unless he asked.

"Did you and the other kid have to do a job?"

Fred dried his hands. "Yeah, Mr. Dickinson made us work."

"Good idea. You mess up, you clean up."

Fred wanted to say, but what if you weren't the person who made the mess? Mr. Dickinson hadn't really accused him of doing it, but there was no use in trying to make his father believe him. Because of the trouble he'd had with the shrimp, everyone accused him.

Using a wooden stirring spoon, his dad filled two large bowls with canned stew. He took them to the table.

They sat down and ate without saying a word. Even when his mom had been at home his father never talked much at supper time, so why would he say anything now?

Finally his dad said, "I guess we all make mistakes."

Not sure exactly whose or what mistake his dad was talking about, Fred didn't reply.

The minutes dragged on and Fred kept chewing on the tasty bits of meat in the stew and using his bread to soak up the juice.

His dad put down his coffee mug. "When I was a kid, I got into trouble at school, too. But I saw I'd done wrong and I corrected it. You can learn from your mistakes."

"I can. I will." He hoped his dad understood a little about his problems.

"Good." His dad finished his supper. "I don't want the principal calling here again." He raised his eyebrows. "Is that clear?"

"He won't." Fred let out his breath. His dad wasn't really mad at him. He'd try and improve. Miss Clark even said he had lots of good qualities, and he'd show her that she was right.

After cleaning the kitchen, Fred grabbed his back pack from the hall and headed for his bedroom. He unzipped the bag and dumped the contents on his bed.

Great, tonight he'd work on all his new ideas.

CHAPTER TWELVE

Greg reported to the office after school at the same time as the Barbarian and they sat side-by-side on two chairs in the waiting area. Determined not to get into any more trouble or even look sideways at the Barbarian, Greg stared at the high counter in front of the secretary's desk.

Mr. Dickinson strode into the office. "Ready to work, boys?"

"Yes," replied Greg and Fred together.

Once they were in the bathroom, Mr. Dickinson inspected the walls. "Looks fine. You both did a good job this morning. We'll start with the edging at the top." He took off his jacket and put on an old shirt and then positioned the ladder near the wall. "It's a little beyond your reach so I'll do the cutting in along the top. You can open the tin for me, Greg."

Greg pried the lid.

"Careful," warned Mr. Dickinson. "The can is really full and easy to spill."

Greg eased the lid off and laid it on some newspapers.

The principal poured a little paint into the tray, balanced it on the holder and climbed the ladder. He dipped the tip of the brush into the paint and edged along the top of the wall. When he'd finished he said, "Fred, you remove the tray while Greg and I shift the ladder."

The Barbarian lifted the tray and held it as Greg helped the principal.

"It won't take me long to finish the edging and then you can start on the walls," said the principal.

He'd just started when the secretary's voice rang over the PA system. "Mr. Dickinson, could you please come to the office."

He stepped down. "I'll be back in a few minutes. Don't do anything. Wait here for me."

Greg braced his hand on a partition near the exit. He didn't want to sit, where he'd have to look up. At least if he stood, he could run faster if the Barbarian decided to start a fight.

He wondered how long it'd take to paint the wall. Why was Mr. Dickinson so slow? The Barbarian shuffled and started pacing, like a caged animal. But after a few minutes he stopped. Greg cringed. By the wild look on the Barbarian's face, he wasn't sure if the guy wanted a fight.

"How long do you figure we'll have to wait?" asked Greg.

The Barbarian hunched his shoulders. "How am I supposed to know?"

He wasn't any help so Greg tried another question. "I don't want to be here all night. Do you?"

"No."

Boy, this was the first time he'd ever tried talking to the Barbarian and the guy wasn't making it very easy. He tried again. "What if we get started?"

When the Barbarian didn't answer, Greg continued, "I mean, the sooner we get to work the faster we'll be done. Right?"

Greg had never seen the Barbarian want to do much except cause trouble and he didn't seem too excited about starting the job, so Greg climbed the ladder and said, "I'll finish up here."

Following the principal's method, he carefully dipped the end of the brush and then tapped it against the side of the tray. Holding the ladder with his left hand, he stretched and painted to the far right.

Once he'd finished part of the wall, he stepped down, feeling pleased with himself. "Hey, it's not hard."

The Barbarian stood next to a sink, not saying a word. Greg waited for a reply but after a few minutes he grew tired so he said, "Help me push the ladder. Okay?"

The Barbarian gripped the rungs and started to pull.

"Easy. We don't want to spill any paint." He indicated the tray that was still attached.

Slowly and gently they dragged it.

"A little more. Watch the floor. It's bumpy near the drain," warned Greg.

Once again Greg climbed the ladder but this time the job wasn't as simple. A pipe jutted out near the ceiling and he had to brush around it. Stretching even farther, he pushed his leg against a rung for more support. Metal squeaked. Greg shifted and tried to balance as the ladder wobbled and tipped away. Attempting to steady himself, he bumped his hand and the paint brush flew into the air. He lurched sideways and clutched at the wall, trying to stop his fall, but his outstretched hands slid down the smooth surface and he thumped on the floor.

"Aaahhhh." The cry bounced off the walls.

The Barbarian lunged to catch the tray, but missed and stumbled. The ladder rattled and crashed. Paint splashed and the tray plonked upside-down.

Green rivers streamed towards the drain.

"Jeez, my foot's caught." The Barbarian twisted, trying to untangle himself.

Greg shook himself and sat up. He wasn't hurt but a horrible thought struck him. What would the Barbarian do once he got up? "I…I'm sorry," he muttered as he up-righted the tray.

The Barbarian didn't reply. Paint splattered his hair and face and ran down his cheeks. Greg shivered as a drop landed on the Barbarian's shirt collar.

"I've gotta get out of here," said the Barbarian, his huge body unfolding like some monster rising out of a swampy, bubbling, dirty green lake. And by the look in monster's eyes, Greg knew if he said anything now he'd really get pounded.

The Barbarian scowled and seemed, for the first time, to sense the sticky wetness on his cheek. He wiped it with his shirt sleeve. "What's this?"

"Y…you've got some s… stuff on you," stuttered Greg.

A drop plinked on the tip on the Barbarian's nose. "Yuck." He glared.

Greg's heart hammered so hard he thought it'd burst out of his chest.

The Barbarian grunted and lumbered to his feet, his face smeared in green and snorting like some creature from another world.

Greg cringed, feeling like a mouse ready to be attacked upon by a monster cat.

"Boo?" The Barbarian jumped and waved his arms.

"N…no." Greg put his hands up to protect his head and shuffled towards the wall, wondering how he'd escape.

"Boo, boo." Drops of paint flung from the Barbarian and he raised his hands, fingers spread, like two giant claws ready to rip Greg apart.

Suddenly the huge figure towering above Greg seemed funny. He snickered and pointed to the Barbarian's face. "It's all over you. You look like a swamp monster." Greg clamped his hand over his mouth, surprised at his words.

The Barbarian snorted again and more paint sprayed his shirt, but instead of pounding him, the Barbarian laughed, making Greg laugh harder, double over and hold his sides.

"There's paint on you, too. We're in big trouble," said the Barbarian.

"We've got to clean up." Paint dripped down the wall and small streams trickled to the drain. Greg had no idea what Mr. Dickinson would do to them if he saw the mess. And he didn't want to find out.

"Why don't we use those rags?" Greg pointed to a pile in the corner. He picked up a cloth and rubbed the spots on his clothes. "Come on, hurry."

The Barbarian didn't move and Greg wondered if he'd get clobbered now.

"You've got to get the guck out of your hair," said Greg.

The Barbarian touched his head and rubbed his sticky fingers. He bent over the sink, turned on the tap and plunged his head under the running water.

"Want me to help?" Greg offered.

The Barbarian mumbled something which Greg took as yes, so he soaped his palms and scrubbed the Barbarian's head, like his mom used to do with him when he was little. Never in a million years did he ever think he'd be doing this. Things sure turned out weird.

"Give me a towel," said Fred as he lifted his head.

"Stop, I'm not finished."

The Barbarian didn't argue. He stuck his head back in the sink and groped for the taps.

Greg checked that the water wasn't too hot. He scrubbed the Barbarian's head some more and finally rinsed the soap out. "I think it's okay. I'll get you a towel."

As he picked up one of the better-looking rags for the Barbarian, he saw that the drips of paint clung to the walls. "We'd better hurry and get this wiped off before it dries," said Greg, as he handed the Barbarian a towel.

"Right, you do the floor and I'll do the walls." The Barbarian picked up a cloth and started dabbing.

Greg mopped up the sticky pools. "Hurry. It's drying fast."

Scrambling back and forth to the sink with dirty rags that he rinsed and squeezed, Greg forgot all about his enemy as they worked together.

Finally the bathroom was clean, but the painting job still wasn't finished.

Greg glanced at his watch, "Wow, it's five o'clock. Do you think Mr. Dickinson's forgotten us?"

"I don't know," said the Barbarian as he hung the last rag over the sink to dry. "Let's find out."

Greg stepped out of the bathroom and spotted the principal coming down the hall.

"I'm sorry to have kept you waiting. The call took a lot longer than I expected." He scrutinized them. "Is everything okay?"

"Yeah, sure." Both boys nodded.

"Good. We won't be able to get on with the job tonight. It's too late. You may go home."

Greg breathed out and hurried to the exit. He'd been lucky. It'd been his idea not to wait for the principal so it was kind of his fault for the mess. He hadn't believed the Barbarian would help him. He didn't have to.

Greg chuckled, recalling the Barbarian with green paint dripping from his hair. He pictured a creature with green slime hanging from its body as it climbed out of a misty lake.

A new idea grabbed him. Tonight, he'd create Swamp Monster, but this time the drawing wouldn't look anything like the Barbarian.

CHAPTER THIRTEEN

Tick, tock, tick, tock. The clock on the kitchen wall beat a steady rhythm and for the hundredth time Fred glanced at it and wondered when his dad would get home from work.

A low rumbling belch escaped from his stomach. "Ugh," he gagged and slapped his hand over his mouth. "I'll never eat donuts and pop for supper again."

Bang! He smacked his hand on the table. "Why don't you come home, Dad?" But he knew the answer. He'd still be at the office working, bent over his desk and only thinking about his job.

"Oh, Mom. Where are you?" His head pounded and he sniffed. Wiping his nose with the back of his hand, he remembered the last time he'd seen her. There'd been tears in her eyes as she'd kissed him, and he'd pulled away from her when she said, "I know it's difficult, Fred, but I have to leave. Have faith that one day I'll return for you." Her voice had cracked and she'd stopped talking. But her eyes had pleaded with him to understand.

"I don't believe you! I hate you!" he'd shouted back at her. The words rang in his mind. He picked up a glass from the side of the sink and drank some water to ease his throat.

"Why did I say that to you? Will you ever come back to Dad and me?"

Through his tears he could still see her red coat as she trudged down the front sidewalk with a suitcase in each hand. As the cab pulled into the street she'd opened the window and peered out. Not wanting her to see him, he'd dropped the bedroom curtain and moved away from the window and huddled in a corner.

It seemed like such a long time ago now, since he and his dad had moved to a new city and to this old house and the awful school where nobody liked him and one kid drew pictures of him and everyone believed he was stupid and ugly.

"I don't really hate you Mom and I want you to keep writing to me even if I never write back." Fred paused and remembered the letters she'd sent him. They'd all been signed, Love Mom, but he'd hardly bothered to read them. Mostly he'd ripped them into little pieces and stuffed them into the bottom of the garbage pail. But he'd kept the last two and hidden them under some socks in his dresser.

"Oh, Mom, I love you and I want you to know." Deciding what he'd do, Fred raced to his bedroom to get a piece of paper.

***

A steady ringing noise woke Fred and he sat up in bed. His dad's voice sounded through the open bedroom door as he talked on the phone.

"Good evening, Mr. Dickinson."

Fred propped himself up on his elbow, trying to hear. He must really be in trouble or the principal wouldn't be calling so late. Today, when he'd left school, he thought everything was okay. After school he'd finished painting the bathroom with Greg. What'd he done wrong now?

What if his marks weren't good enough and he'd fail. He couldn't hear the words until his father said, "Yes, thank you for calling me." The phone clicked.

Fred pulled up the blankets and covered his shoulders, rolled to face the wall and scrunched down, pretending he was asleep.

The sound of breathing warned Fred that his father stood beside the bed.

"Goodnight, son." The door closed quietly.

Fred wondered if he'd heard right. His dad didn't seem mad or anything. Probably he'd get lectured in the morning, and once again be in big trouble.

CHAPTER FOURTEEN

As Greg opened the door and eased out of his backpack he heard his mom's voice in the living room.

"Oh, Jennifer, it's been wonderful to hear from you after all these years. We'll have to get together."

He grabbed an apple from the bowl on the counter and leaned against the cupboard, straining to hear his mom's words.

She came into the kitchen with the phone pressed to her ear and waved at him. "I must go now. My son is here giving me a funny look and it's time for supper. Talk to you soon." She replaced the phone in the cradle.

"Who's Jennifer?" asked Greg.

"An old friend of mine. We go way back to high school and I haven't talked to her in years. It's wonderful to be in touch with her again."

"Hey, you know the contest?" Greg blurted, not really interested in some lady his mom knew a long time ago.

His mom took lettuce out of the fridge. "Do you mean the art contest?"

"Yeah, well... I don't think I'm going to win."

His mom placed the lettuce on the counter and took some tomatoes out of a bowl. "Why do you say that?"

"When I handed in my cartoons I saw some other drawings in the contest pile and they were super good."

His mom chopped the tomatoes. "Oh, really. What were they like?"

"Dragon drawings of all different shapes and sizes." At school he talked to Miss Clark in the hall and she'd told him to put his portfolio on her desk. In the classroom he'd seen another folder on her desk. It looked like someone's art so he'd peeked inside. There was no name, only a number. He figured it had to be another entry for the contest.

"Well..." His mom paused. "You never know what the judges will think. You don't know what they're looking for. Your cartoons are totally original."

"But Mom. These were really good." He took a big bite from the apple.

"You might think that because they were something different and interesting."

"You don't understand."

His mom stopped chopping the tomatoes and faced him. "I'm listening, so tell me."

"The drawings had lots of details. The scales and claws were perfect and I'll never win the contest." Greg hung his head.

"If you have that attitude, you won't win." His mom's voice was sharp.

"But my cartoons look so silly. The judges will like the dragons better."

His mom put her hands on her hips and glared at him, like she did when he'd done something wrong. "And how do you know? I'm sure the judges are knowledgeable artists and they'll recognize good art work no matter if it's dragons or cartoons."

"Maybe." Greg considered. "You don't know how much I want to win."

"Most of us want to win, but it often doesn't happen in life, so you might as well get used to it. Think of the other person. He or she probably wants the prize as much as you."

Greg shuffled to table and plopped on the chair. "I don't think so."

"Win or lose, when the award is presented I want you to be a good sport and congratulate the winner, whoever it is."

Gee, why was his mom always so nice to other people? But maybe she was right. Maybe another person loved art as much as he did.

"Think about it this way, honey, there will be other places for you to show your art and if you love doing it you won't stop because of one contest you win or don't win."

"Yeah, maybe," said Greg. "I don't know, I'll think about it."

CHAPTER FIFTEEN

On the last day of school and the graduating ceremony for all sixth-graders, Greg sat on the wooden risers, with the rest of his classmates, at the front of the gym. Students entered and sat on the floor. Chairs lined the back of the room and parents quickly filled them. Greg peered at the crowd, trying to see his mom.

The room buzzed with adults and kids talking.

In the next hour Mr. Dickinson would announce the winner of the art contest. Greg crossed his fingers. Maybe he'd win the prize, but a little inner voice told him that whoever drew the dragon pictures would probably win.

Once more Greg scanned the back of the gym, looking for his mom. Ah. There she was, walking through the door and talking to a woman in a red coat. Greg frowned. Who was the lady? He'd never seen her before. They stopped, checked for empty seats, and squeezed down a row.

Mr. Dickinson stepped to the microphone and the chatter from the crowd stopped. "Welcome parents, students and teachers." He paused and turned. "And a special welcome to our sixth-graders who will be performing at today's assembly. Let's all stand and begin by singing our national anthem."

After the shuffling of chairs and the movement of feet stopped the entire assembly stood at attention.

At the end of the song everyone sat down. For the first part of the program the sixth- graders sang some songs and when they finished, Mr. Dickinson stepped back to the mike. "It is our school custom, at this time, to honor one or two students who have demonstrated what it means to be a good citizen. These are our citizenship awards." He paused and Greg felt that every kid was holding his breath, hoping to win. But Greg knew for sure he wouldn't, not after the trouble he'd had with the Barbarian. The award didn't go to anyone who had to paint the boys' bathroom and scrub the lunchroom. He wished the principal would hurry up and get to the art contest.

Mr. Dickinson walked to the table on the other side of the gym and held up a trophy. "At this time I have the great pleasure to announce the names of the two students who have shown what it means to be a good citizen. This year our winners are…" he paused.

Greg expected some drum rolls; instead everyone held his breath and everyone's eyes were on Mr. Dickinson as he said, This year's winners are Angela Archer and Tommy Brownlee. Would they please come forward."

Before he knew it, Greg clapped and cheered along with the rest of the people. Angela's face got redder as she stepped down from the risers.

In his enthusiasm, Tommy jumped over the last step and clunked on the floor, almost tripping. The audience laughed and applauded even louder. Cameras clicked and flashed as parents took pictures with Angela and Tommy holding the large trophy.

After the noise subsided, Mr. Dickinson cleared his throat. "One of the highlights of this term has been a city-wide art contest. No doubt parents have heard about it from their son or daughter. As I'm sure you are aware, first prize is a gift certificate allowing the winner to purchase art supplies to continue his or her work. I'm delighted to announce that this year's winner comes from our school."

A collective 'ah' came from the audience and they hushed.

"To accept the 'World of Art' gift certificate would the winner, Fred Farley, please come forward."

Sitting in the top row of the risers, Fred's mind went blank. He gawked at the principal. Mr. Dickinson had said his name. Hadn't he? At least that's what he thought he'd heard. But everyone was sure Greg would win.

"Get up there. You won," someone close by whispered.

The pounding in his chest got worse and his legs felt like jelly. Fred glanced around, his face getting hot. All eyes were on him. The room blurred and the principal raised his hand.

Through the hum of voices, Fred heard, "Yes, Fred, *you* are the winner."

He pushed himself up, stepped down and walked to the side of the gym.

Everyone applauded and the principal shook his hand and gave him a white envelope and said, "Congratulations, Fred. Your drawings are excellent."

Cameras flashed, blinding Fred. Mr. Dickinson's hand rested on his shoulder. "Smile, Fred, so you take a good picture." After the pictures were taken the principal said, "Now go and stand beside Angela and Tommy."

Clutching the envelope tight, Fred walked to where they were standing.

Greg's mouth dropped open. He'd been right; the dragon drawings had won the contest. But who would have ever guessed the Barbarian had drawn them?

The noise stopped and Mr. Dickinson started to speak again. "At this time, I have the pleasure of announcing another prize. The local artists who judged the contest were impressed with the quality of not one but two artists. They realize each one has a unique talent. Therefore, there will be a special award to another student, who will take lessons from a professional artist during the summer holidays."

Greg's head shot up and he crossed his fingers. Did he… would his name be called?

He shot a glance at the other students and saw the snarl on Jason's face and Greg knew who'd written on the bathroom wall, but right now it didn't matter.

The principal said, "Our other winner is well known for his little cartoon drawings."

Greg held his breath as he waited for the next words.

"Please come forward to accept your award. Greg Hutchins."

The next thing Greg knew the principal shook his hand and everybody clapped. He looked to the back of the gym. His mom stood beside the lady in the red coat.

Remembering what she'd said, he stretched out his hand to the Barbarian and said, "Congratulations."

The Barbarian grabbed his hand and shook it, just like they'd always been best buddies.

Greg couldn't believe it. The Barbarian smiled. The biggest Greg had ever seen. Was his mom right? The Barbarian seemed to care, so Greg smiled back.

Mr. Dickinson stood behind the four winners and said, "Face the audience once more."

Greg let go of the Barbarian's hand and turned to the audience. Today was the start of the summer holidays and best day of the whole year.

Fred grasped the envelope in his left hand and faced the flashing cameras and cheering people. Everything blurred and the applause seemed to get even louder. He straightened and squinted as he stared at the back of the gym. In the sea of color and sound he saw someone he knew. Someone he longed to see. A red coat. But it couldn't be. No, he'd hoped so long for this. She waved.

Fred blinked to make sure he wasn't imagining. She was still there and all he wanted to do was run and hug her and tell her how much he missed her and how much he loved her.

Fred swallowed, still not sure it was happening to him. He'd won the art contest and all the students had cheered and clapped for him. Even the shrimp, Greg, had said congratulations, like he meant it. But the best thing of all, the thing that made him feel so good inside. His mom had finally come back to him and he hoped they'd be a family again.

ANOTHER NOVEL BY SHERILE REILLY IS AVAILABLE. SPUNKY: TAPPING INTO TROUBLE

Tap dancing and riding her dilapidated bike are ten-year-old Sarah Crawford's, better known as Spunky, favorite activities. After moving to Badger Creek with her mom, Spunky discovers the old lady in the basement apartment dislikes both her and her dancing.

Accused of being too noisy and stealing, Spunky discovers her troubles are just beginning.

CPSIA information can be obtained at www.ICGtesting.com
Printed in the USA
LVOW07s0753181114

414156LV00003B/20/P